Herbster Readers

THE HALLOWEEN COSTUME CONTEST

Written by Cecilia Minden and Joanne Meier • Illustrated by Bob Ostrom
Created by Herbie J. Thorpe

ABOUT THE AUTHORS

Cecilia Minden, PhD, is the former director of the Language and Literacy Program at the Harvard Graduate School of Education. She is now a reading consultant for school and library publications. She earned her PhD in reading education from the University of Virginia. Cecilia and her husband, Dave Cupp, live outside Chapel Hill, North Carolina. They enjoy sharing their love of reading with their grandchildren, Chelsea and Qadir.

Joanne Meier, PhD, has worked as an elementary school teacher, university professor, and researcher. She earned her BA in early childhood education from the University of South Carolina, and her MEd and PhD in education from the University of Virginia. She currently works as a literacy consultant for schools and private organizations. Joanne lives in Virginia with her husband Eric, daughters Kella and Erin, two cats, and a gerbil.

ABOUT THE ILLUSTRATOR

Bob Ostrom has been illustrating children's books for nearly twenty years. A graduate of the New England School of Art & Design at Suffolk University, Bob has worked for such companies as Disney, Nickelodeon, and Cartoon Network. He lives in North Carolina with his wife Melissa and three children, Will, Charlie, and Mae.

ABOUT THE SERIES CREATOR

Herbie J. Thorpe had long envisioned a beginning-readers' series about a fun, energetic bear with a big imagination. Herbie is a book lover and an avid supporter of libraries and the role they play in fostering the love of reading. He consults with librarians and matches them with the perfect books for their students and patrons. He lives in Louisiana with his wife Misty and their daughter Carson.

The Child's World®

Published in the United States of America by The Child's World®
1980 Lookout Drive • Mankato, MN 56003-1705
800-599-READ • www.childsworld.com

Acknowledgments
The Child's World®: Mary Berendes, Publishing Director
The Design Lab: Kathleen Petelinsek, Design;
Kari Tobin, Page Production
Artistic Assistant: Richard Carbajal

Library of Congress Cataloging-in-Publication Data
Minden, Cecilia.
  The Halloween costume contest / by Cecilia Minden and Joanne Meier ; illustrated by Bob Ostrom.
    p. cm. — (Herbster readers)
  ISBN 978-1-60253-217-5 (library bound : alk. paper)
  [1. Halloween—Fiction. 2. Costume—Fiction. 3. Bears—Fiction.] I. Meier, Joanne D. II. Ostrom, Bob, ill. III. Title. IV. Series.

  PZ7.M6539Hal 2009
  [E]—dc22   2009003979

HALLOWEEN COSTUME CONTEST

Herbie Bear's school was having a Halloween costume contest.

"Let's dress up like pirates," said Michael.

5

"We could wear eye patches."

"We were pirates last year.

We didn't win," said Herbie.

"We could be knights," said Herbie.

"Charlie was a knight last year.

He didn't win," said Michael.

"I'm hungry," said Herbie.

"Let's have a snack."

"Peanut butter is good for everything," said Herbie.

Herbie looked at Michael.

"I have an idea!" said Herbie.

HALLOWEEN COSTUME CONTEST

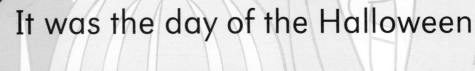

It was the day of the Halloween costume contest.

There were so many costumes!

Ken was a cowboy.

Kim was a princess.

Mrs. Zazu and Mr. Clark were the judges.
"Everyone looks wonderful," they said.

"The winners are Herbie and Michael!" said Mrs. Zazu.

Herbie and Michael came to the stage.

The crowd cheered!

"You were right," said Michael.

"Peanut butter *is* good for everything."

Herbie just smiled.